Fox in Socks

By
Dr. Seuss

HarperCollins *Children's Books*

For
Mitzi Long and Audrey Dimond
of the
Mt. Soledad Lingual Laboratories

19 20 18

ISBN-10: 0-00-715847-5
ISBN-13: 978-0-00-715847-8

A Beginner Book published by arrangement with
Random House Inc., New York, USA
First published in the UK 1966
This edition published in the UK 2003 by
HarperCollins*Children's Books*,
a division of HarperCollins*Publishers* Ltd
77-85 Fulham Palace Road
London W6 8JB

Visit our website at:
www.harpercollins.co.uk

Printed and bound in Hong Kong

Fox in Socks

Fox

Socks

Box

Knox

3

Knox in box.
Fox in socks.

Knox on fox
in socks in box.

Socks on Knox
and Knox in box.

Fox in socks
on box on Knox.

Chicks with bricks come.
Chicks with blocks come.
Chicks with bricks and
blocks and clocks come.

Look, sir. Look, sir.
Mr. Knox, sir.
Let's do tricks with
bricks and blocks, sir.
Let's do tricks with
chicks and clocks, sir.

First, I'll make a
quick trick brick stack.
Then I'll make a
quick trick block stack.

You can make a
quick trick chick stack.
You can make a
quick trick clock stack.

And here's a
new trick, Mr. Knox. . . .
Socks on chicks
and chicks on fox.
Fox on clocks
on bricks and blocks.
Bricks and blocks
on Knox on box.

Now we come to
ticks and tocks, sir.
Try to say this
Mr. Knox, sir. . . .

Clocks on fox tick.
Clocks on Knox tock.
Six sick bricks tick.
Six sick chicks tock.

Please, sir. I don't
like this trick, sir.
My tongue isn't
quick or slick, sir.
I get all those
ticks and clocks, sir,
mixed up with the
chicks and tocks, sir.
I can't do it, Mr. Fox, sir.

I'm so sorry,
Mr. Knox, sir.

17

Here's an easy
game to play.
Here's an easy
thing to say. . . .

New socks.
Two socks.
Whose socks?
Sue's socks.

Who sews whose socks?
Sue sews Sue's socks.

Who sees who sew
whose new socks, sir?
You see Sue sew
Sue's new socks, sir.

That's not easy,
Mr. Fox, sir.

Who comes? . . .
Crow comes.
Slow Joe Crow comes.

Who sews crow's clothes?
Sue sews crow's clothes.
Slow Joe Crow
sews whose clothes?
Sue's clothes.

Sue sews socks of
fox in socks now.

Slow Joe Crow sews
Knox in box now.

Sue sews rose
on Slow Joe Crow's clothes.
Fox sews hose
on Slow Joe Crow's nose.

Hose goes.
Rose grows.
Nose hose goes some.
Crow's rose grows some.

Mr. Fox!
I hate this game, sir.
This game makes
my tongue quite lame, sir.

28

Mr. Knox, sir,
what a shame, sir.

We'll find something
new to do now.
Here is lots of
new blue goo now.
New goo. Blue goo.
Gooey. Gooey.
Blue goo. New goo.
Gluey. Gluey.

Gooey goo
for chewy chewing!
That's what that
Goo-Goose is doing.
Do you choose to
chew goo, too, sir?
If, sir, you, sir,
choose to chew, sir,
with the Goo-Goose,
chew, sir. Do, sir.

Mr. Fox, sir,
I won't do it.
I can't say it.
I won't chew it.

Very well, sir.
Step this way.
We'll find another
game to play.

Bim comes.
Ben comes.
Bim brings Ben broom.
Ben brings Bim broom.

Ben bends Bim's broom.
Bim bends Ben's broom.
Bim's bends.
Ben's bends.
Ben's bent broom breaks.
Bim's bent broom breaks.

Ben's band. Bim's band.
Big bands. Pig bands.

BOOM

Bim and Ben lead
bands with brooms.
Ben's band bangs
and Bim's band booms.

Pig band! Boom band!
Big band! Broom band!
My poor mouth can't
say that. No, sir.
My poor mouth is
much too slow, sir.

Well then . . .
bring your mouth this way.
I'll find it something
it can say.

Luke Luck likes lakes.
Luke's duck likes lakes.
Luke Luck licks lakes.
Luke's duck licks lakes.

Duck takes licks
in lakes Luke Luck likes.
Luke Luck takes licks
in lakes duck likes.

I can't blab
such blibber blubber!
My tongue isn't
made of rubber.

Mr. Knox. Now
come now. Come now.
You don't have to
be so dumb now. . . .

Try to say this,
Mr. Knox, please. . . .

Through three cheese trees
three free fleas flew.
While these fleas flew,
freezy breeze blew.
Freezy breeze made
these three trees freeze.
Freezy trees made
these trees' cheese freeze.
That's what made these
three free fleas sneeze.

Stop it! Stop it!
That's enough, sir.
I can't say
such silly stuff, sir.

Very well, then,
Mr. Knox, sir.

Let's have a little talk
about tweetle beetles. . . .

What do you know
about tweetle beetles?
Well . . .

When tweetle beetles fight,
it's called
a tweetle beetle battle.

And when they
battle in a puddle,
it's a tweetle
beetle puddle battle.

AND when tweetle beetles
battle with paddles in a puddle,
they call it a tweetle
beetle puddle paddle battle.
                    AND . . .

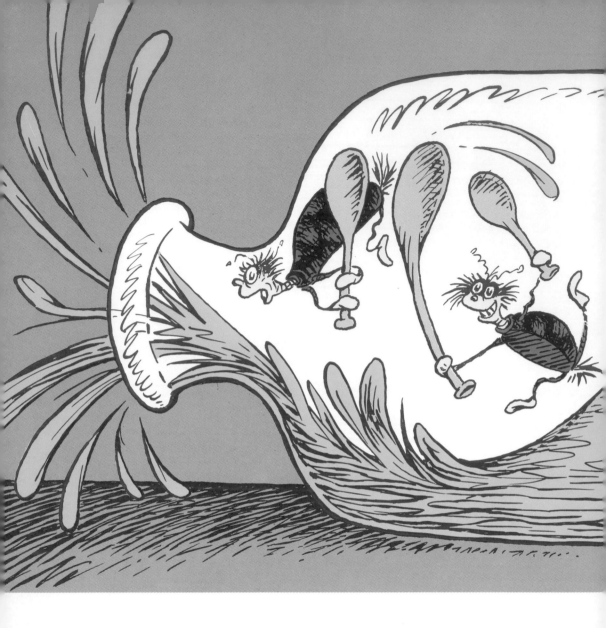

When beetles battle beetles
in a puddle paddle battle
and the beetle battle puddle
is a puddle in a bottle . . .

. . . they call this
a tweetle beetle
bottle puddle
paddle battle muddle.
AND . . .

When beetles
fight these battles
in a bottle
with their paddles
and the bottle's
on a poodle
and the poodle's
eating noodles . . .

. . . they call this
a muddle puddle
tweetle poodle
beetle noodle
bottle paddle battle.

AND . . .

Now wait
a minute,
Mr. Socks Fox!

When a fox is
in the bottle where
the tweetle beetles battle
with their paddles
in a puddle on a
noodle-eating poodle,
THIS is what they call . . .

. . . a tweetle beetle
noodle poodle bottled
paddled muddled duddled
fuddled wuddled
fox in socks, sir!

Fox in socks,
our game is done, sir.
Thank you for
a lot of fun, sir.

Dr.Seuss™

The more that you **read,**
the more things **you** will know.
The more that you **learn,**
the **more** places you'll go!

– I Can Read With My Eyes Shut!

With over **35 paperbacks to collect** there's a book for all ages and reading
abilities, and now there's never been a better time to have **fun** with **Dr.Seuss!**
Simply collect 5 tokens from the back of each Dr.Seuss book and send in for your

FREE Dr.Seuss poster

(rrp £3.99)

Send your 5 tokens and a completed voucher to:
Dr. Seuss poster offer, PO Box 142, Horsham, UK, RH13 5FJ (UK residents only)

Title: Mr ☐   Mrs ☐   Miss ☐   Ms ☐

First Name:.. Surname:.............................

Address:..

Post Code:.............................. E-Mail Address:................................

Date of Birth:.......................... Signature of parent/guardian:...............

TICK HERE IF YOU DO NOT WISH TO RECEIVE FURTHER INFORMATION ABOUT CHILDREN'S BOOKS ☐

TERMS AND CONDITIONS: Proof of sending cannot be considered proof of receipt. Not redeemable for cash.
Please allow 28 days for delivery. Photocopied tokens not accepted. Offer open to UK only.

Read them **together**, read them **alone**, read them **aloud** and make **reading fun!**
With over **30 wacky stories** to choose from, now it's **easier** than **ever** to find the
right **Dr. Seuss** books for your child – just let the **back cover colour** guide you!

Blue back books
for sharing with your child

Dr. Seuss' ABC
The Foot Book
Hop on Pop
Mr. Brown Can Moo! Can You?
One Fish, Two Fish, Red Fish, Blue Fish
There's a Wocket in my Pocket!

Green back books
for children just beginning to read on their own

And to Think That I Saw It on Mulberry Street
The Cat in the Hat
The Cat in the Hat Comes Back
Fox in Socks
Green Eggs and Ham
I Can Read With My Eyes Shut!
I Wish That I Had Duck Feet
Marvin K. Mooney Will You Please Go Now!
Oh, Say Can You Say?
Oh, the Thinks You Can Think!
Ten Apples Up on Top
Wacky Wednesday
Hunches in Bunches
Happy Birthday to YOU

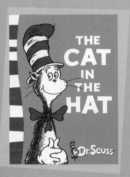

Yellow back books
for fluent readers to enjoy

Daisy-Head Mayzie
Did I Ever Tell You How Lucky You Are?
Dr. Seuss' Sleep Book
Horton Hatches the Egg
Horton Hears a Who!
How the Grinch Stole Christmas!
If I Ran the Circus
If I Ran the Zoo
I Had Trouble in Getting to Solla Sollew
The Lorax
Oh, the Places You'll Go!
On Beyond Zebra
Scrambled Eggs Super!
The Sneetches and other stories
Thidwick the Big-Hearted Moose
Yertle the Turtle and other stories